Dragons Eat Noodles on Tuesdays

BY **Jon Stahl**

ILLUSTRATED BY

Tadgh Bentley

SCHOLASTIC INC.

For Sophie and Charlie,
the best characters
I've ever created.
And for Wendy.
—J.S.

To Freddie and Albie,
from Conkig.

—T.B.

ISBN 978-1-338-53221-0

10 9 8 7 6 5 4 3 2 1   19 20 21 22 23

• PRINTED IN THE U.S.A.   40 • FIRST PRINTING 2019 •

Tadgh Bentley's drawings were created using pencil and pen and were colored with digital gouache and watercolor brushes.
The text type was set in KG Dancing on the Roof Regular. • The display type was set in KG King Cool KC Regular and Tw Cen MT Bold.
Production was overseen by Angie Chen. • Manufacturing was supervised by Shannon Rice.
The book was art directed and designed by Marijka Kostiw, and edited by Dianne Hess.

Like this:

Boy finds toy.

Boy loses toy.

Toy meets girl.

Girl loves toy.

Toy is happy.

Boy gets new toy.

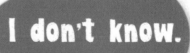

I don't know.

That story really needs a hungry dragon.

Dragon stories usually don't end well. But, if you insist. . . .

I insist.

Okay. But be careful what you wish for.

Once upon a time, a cowardly knight came upon a hungry dragon . . .
P-p-p-leeease don't eat me!
Sorry, pal, I skipped breakfast.
The dragon opened his jaws wide to eat the knight when suddenly . . .

Please, call me Dennis.
Put me down!
I don't care what they call you. You put that knight down, now!
Come on, I'm starving!

But the damsel was not only brave, she was also very smart.
Look, Dennis, everyone knows dragons ONLY eat noodles on Tuesdays!
ye olde dragon menu
monday
knights
tuesday
noodles (only)
wednesday
monsters
thursday
villagers
friday
king buffet
saturday
damsel dinner
sunday
salad

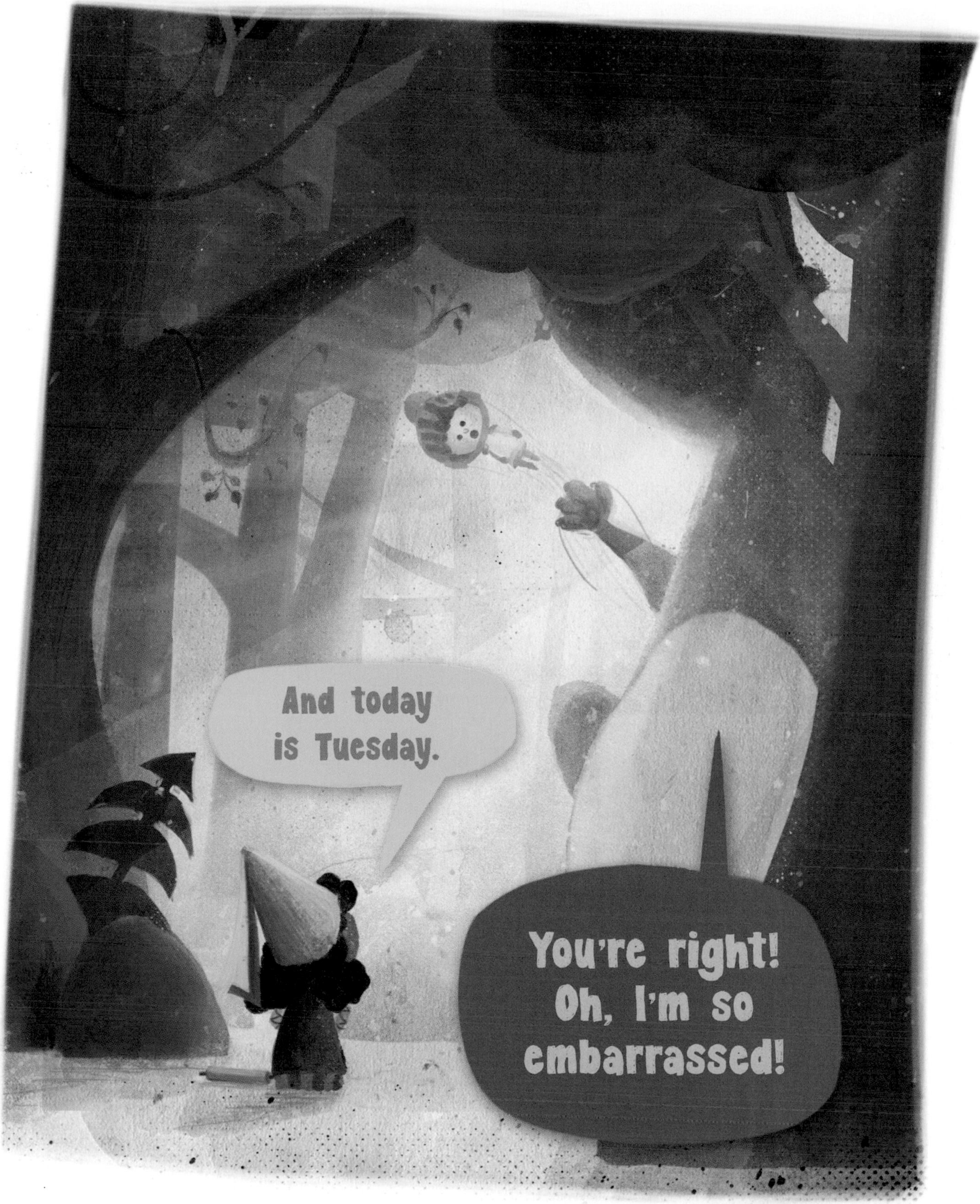
And today is Tuesday.
You're right! Oh, I'm so embarrassed!

That story is ridiculous. Noodles? Come on . . .
I think it's fantastic. You wanted a dragon story.
Hey, what's that?

Oh, no! It looks like Dennis from the story.
Dennis looks hungry.

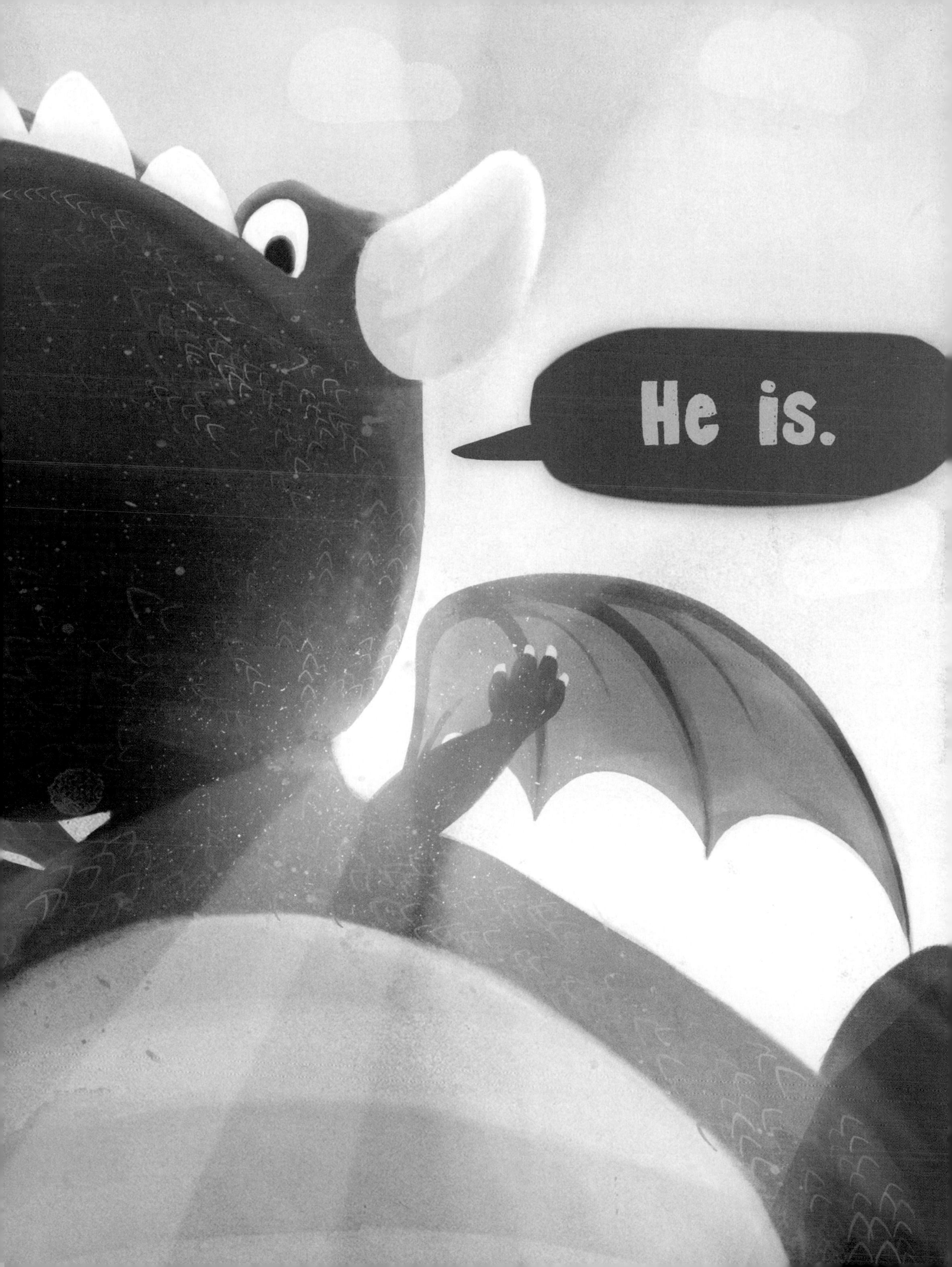
He is.

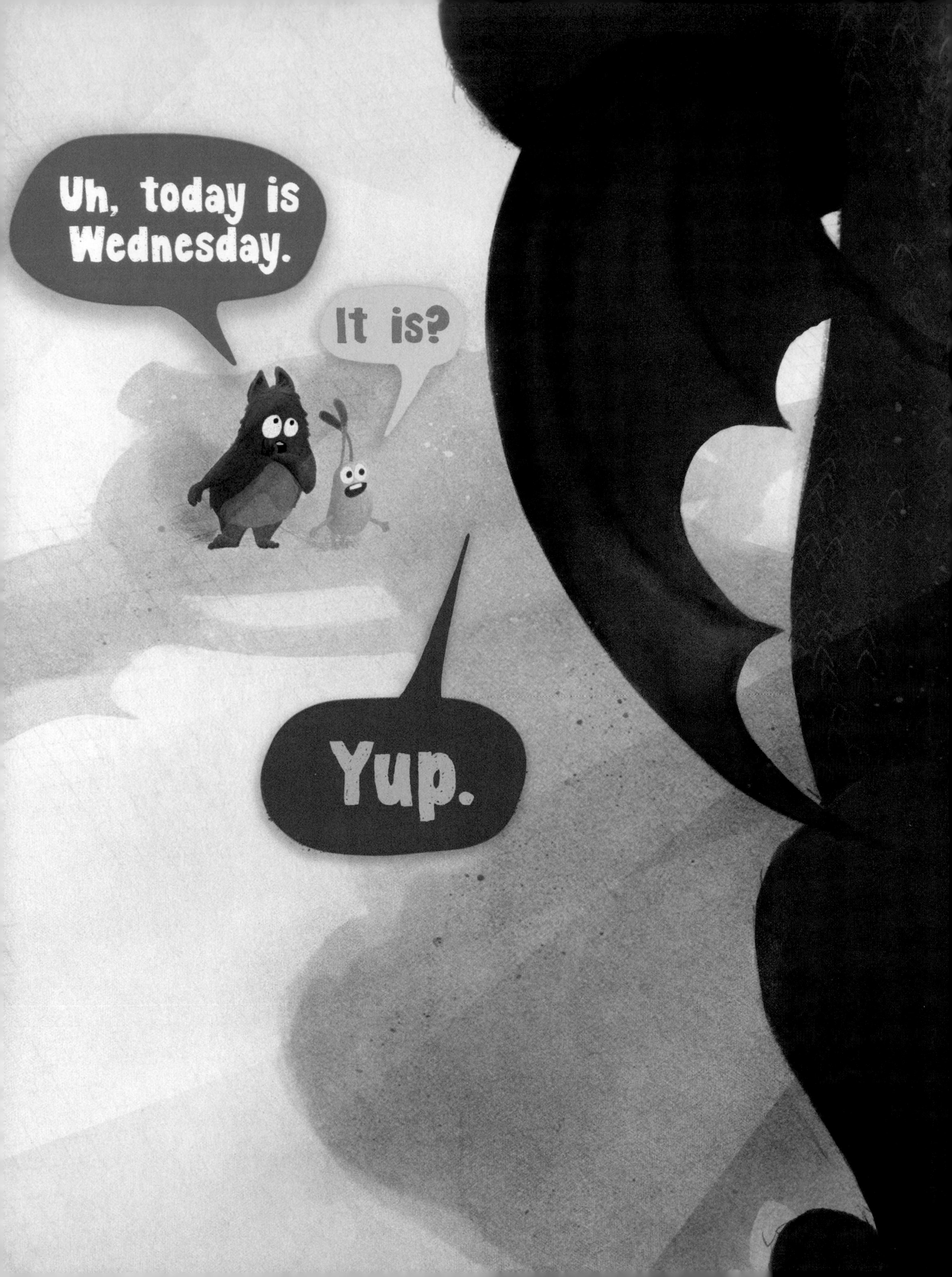
Uh, today is Wednesday.
It is?
Yup.

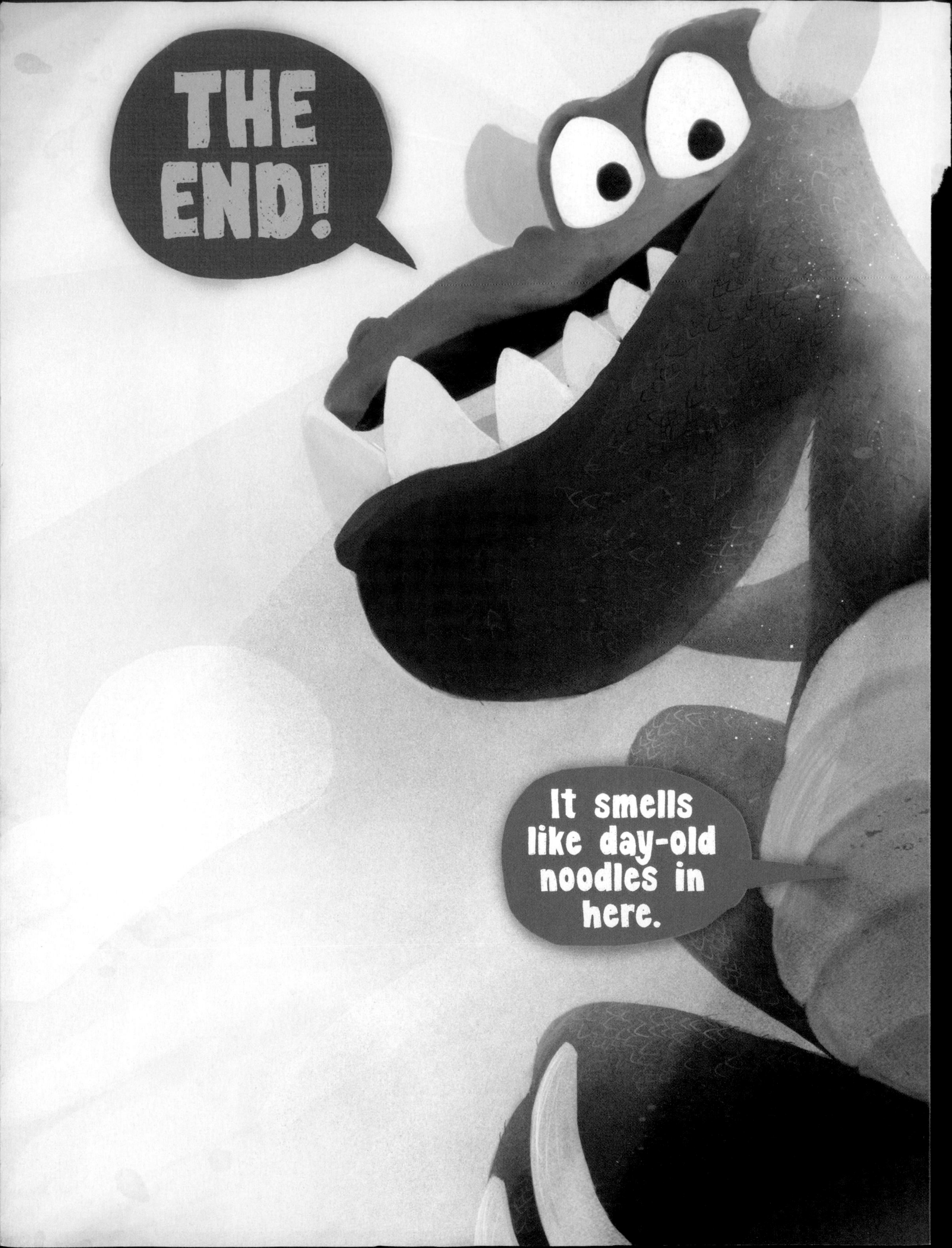
THE END!
It smells like day-old noodles in here.